GROOMING
AND STABLE
MANAGEMENT

Lucy Smith

Designed by Ian McNee
Illustrated by Mikki Rain
Photographs by Kit Houghton
Consultant: Juliet Mander BHSII

Studio photographs by Howard Allman
Edited by Kate Needham
Series Editor: Cheryl Evans

Contents

THE PADDOCK

Keeping a pony is rewarding, but as you will find out in this book, it is also hard work. If you are at school a lot, the cheapest and most practical way for your pony to live, as long as he is hardy, is at pasture. This means he lives in a field or paddock most of the time, where he can roam and graze naturally as he would in the wild.

CARING FOR THE GRASS

Your pony will mainly eat grass while he lives outside. It is a good food, but it needs some care to grow well. Ponies are fussy grazers. They tend to eat all the short, rich grass and leave any that is long, or has manure or urine in it. If they graze a field for too long it gets "horse-sick", with bald patches which they have cropped bare, and other areas full of long, worm-infested grass, where no new shoots can grow.

For one pony, to prevent over-grazing, you need a field of about one hectare (two acres) which you can split into two or three parts. You can then rest two parts while the other is being grazed. Make sure the part the pony grazes has shelter, water and a gate (see opposite). It is also important to clear manure from the field each day. This prevents worms which live in the manure from being eaten by the pony.

DEADLY PLANTS

Remember to check any hedges around the paddock for poisonous plants that the pony might eat.

Before using the paddock, check to see if any poisonous plants are growing there. The types will vary depending on where you live. Ask someone who works with ponies, such as a riding instructor or your vet, for advice about which ones to look for.

Pull up all poisonous plants by the roots and burn them. This will help to stop them from growing again. Get rid of any which the pony could reach over the fence, too.

TYPES OF FENCING

The paddock must be surrounded by a strong, safe fence. This should be at least 1.2m (4ft) high so ponies don't jump out. It needs to be solid enough to take the weight of ponies leaning or rubbing against it. Make sure there are no sharp edges where a pony could cut himself, or gaps where he could escape.

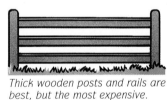

Thick wooden posts and rails are best, but the most expensive.

Dense, trimmed hedges with no deadly plants are good and also give some natural shelter.

Three strands of thick, rust-proof wire strung taut between posts are cheap and effective.

The bottom strand must be at least 30cm (1ft) from the ground, so the pony can't hook his leg in it.

GETTING THE RIGHT GATE

The gate must be hung so that it swings smoothly and shuts firmly. Fit a chain with a padlock as well as the gate fastening, and keep a spare padlock key.

The gateway must be wide enough to let you and your pony through easily side-by-side. Put sand on the ground around the gateway to stop it from getting too muddy.

Ponies are wily and can lift or undo even good gate fastenings like these. You will need a chain and padlock too.

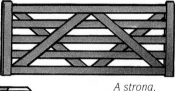

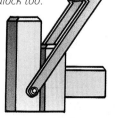

A strong, five-barred wooden or steel gate is best.

PASTURE-KEPT PONIES

Keeping a pony at pasture is a very natural way for him to live, but he won't be able to fend entirely for himself. You will have to supply shelter and fresh water and visit him every morning and evening to make sure he is all right.

THE ADVANTAGES OF A FIELD SHELTER

A field shelter protects your pony from bad weather and is shady in summer. If your pony lives mostly outside, it is also a dry, covered place where you can do a lot of your pony care. On the right is a checklist of the most important features for an ideal shelter.

Shelter checklist
* Three sides.
* Weatherproof roof.
* Back to the windiest part of the paddock.
* Wide opening (so all ponies can get in and out).
* Enough room inside for ponies to lie down or turn around in.
* Dirt floor covered with straw, so ponies can stand or lie down in comfort.
* Nothing sharp or sticking out from the walls, on which a pony could hurt himself.
* A portable manger for any extra food.

FRESH WATER SUPPLY

All ponies need a constant supply of fresh, clean water. In the paddock it is easiest to keep it in a trough which should be long, solid and not too deep. If possible, water should be piped straight to it. Otherwise, empty and refill it each day with buckets of fresh water.

Raise the trough off the ground slightly and put sand down so the grass isn't churned up by hooves.

There should be no sharp edges on the trough. A plug in the bottom means you can drain and clean it.

Put the trough on well-drained land, away from gates or corners where ponies may crowd each other. If the water gets cloudy, empty the trough and scrub it out with a hard brush. Don't use soap or detergents. On frosty winter mornings you may need to break the ice.

DAILY PONY AND PADDOCK CHECK

Feel his ears to check that he is warm. Tie him up. Examine him all over, especially his feet and legs. Deal with wounds at once to stop infections.

Take his blanket off. Check that he is not getting thin on poor pasture in winter, or fat on rich summer grass. Put his blanket back on and untie him afterward.

Check the paddock. Remove rusty wire, tin cans, broken glass, or plastic bags that could choke the pony. Fill in any holes where he might catch his foot.

Clear manure away to keep worms out of the grass. Fork through muck you can't pick up, to let sunlight in. This kills some of the worm eggs.

KEEPING PONIES TOGETHER ON PASTURE

Ponies are much happier in a group. When in a "herd" they quickly work out a pecking order. They may bully a new pony by pushing it around and nipping it with their teeth, as in the paragraph above. Introduce "newcomers" gradually and watch them closely to start with. Be especially careful with very young or old ponies living out in a herd.

Ponies get excited when they smell food, so don't use tidbits to catch a pony on your own if he is out with others. You could be pushed or stepped on as they crowd around.

THE STABLE

Your pony will probably live out most of the time, but you will need a safe, comfortable stable where you can keep him warm if he is not feeling well, or if you need him in tiptop condition to be ready for a show or competition.

THE STABLE BUILDING

A stall in a stable is where the pony can be left untied as long as the door is shut. This means he can move around easily. The stable should have proper drainage, electricity and water, with a faucet nearby for filling buckets. There should be a road so trucks and horse trailers can get to the stable, and you should be able to walk easily from there to the field with the pony.

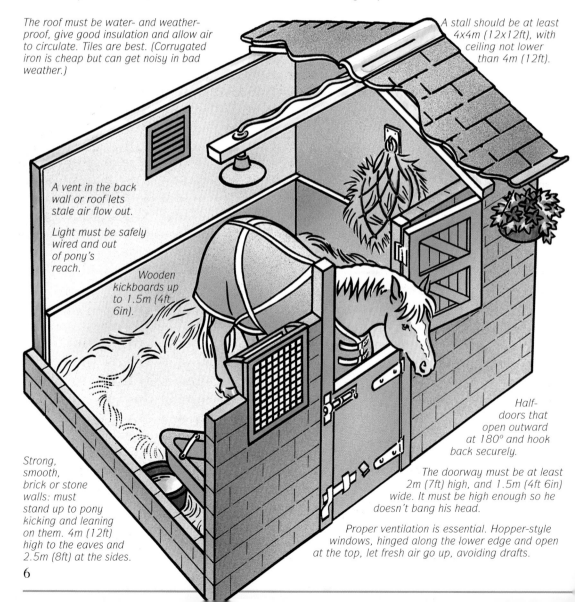

The roof must be water- and weather-proof, give good insulation and allow air to circulate. Tiles are best. (Corrugated iron is cheap but can get noisy in bad weather.)

A stall should be at least 4x4m (12x12ft), with ceiling not lower than 4m (12ft).

A vent in the back wall or roof lets stale air flow out.

Light must be safely wired and out of pony's reach.

Wooden kickboards up to 1.5m (4ft 6in).

Half-doors that open outward at 180° and hook back securely.

Strong, smooth, brick or stone walls: must stand up to pony kicking and leaning on them. 4m (12ft) high to the eaves and 2.5m (8ft) at the sides.

The doorway must be at least 2m (7ft) high, and 1.5m (4ft 6in) wide. It must be high enough so he doesn't bang his head.

Proper ventilation is essential. Hopper-style windows, hinged along the lower edge and open at the top, let fresh air go up, avoiding drafts.

FIXTURES YOU MIGHT NEED

Have as few fixtures in the stall as you can, so they don't take up much room and the pony won't bump into or chew them. Make sure they have no sharp edges and are firmly attached. If possible, put them on the front wall so you don't have to go past the pony each time you feed him.

You need a tethering ring inside, and one outside for tying up the pony. They should be level with the pony's chest.

Put a ring on the outside wall in case you ever want to hang up a haynet for your pony while he waits to be cared for.

The manger should be in one corner, about 1m (3ft 6in) from the floor. Removable ones are easy to fill, empty, and clean.

HOW TO PREVENT A STABLE FIRE

A fire in a stable is one of the worst things that can happen if you keep a pony. Ponies are terrified of fire, so make sure you know exactly what to do if a fire does break out, and take the precautions in the checklist on the right.

Checklist
* Make sure you know how to get your pony out quickly and safely. Have an actual drill, learn it by heart and practice it.
* Keep all supplies of straw and hay away from the stable as these burn very fast.
* Keep fire extinguishers and fire buckets somewhere out of the pony's reach but close at hand.
* Install smoke and fire alarms.
* Don't let anyone smoke around the stable. Put up "No Smoking" signs for visitors.
* Display a fire notice showing the drill, where the alarms and fire extinguishers are, where to meet, and any emergency telephone numbers.
* Practice taking your pony out of his stable safely.

MAINTAINING THE STABLE

Every day	Every week	Every few months
Clean out food and water containers.	Clean windows.	Check gutters, roof, wiring, drains.
Sweep stable area.	Check light bulbs.	Check woodwork for rot or woodworm.
Muck out (see pages 10-11).	Check first aid kit (see page 31) and fire equipment.	Oil hinges, check doors.
Neaten muck heap.	Clean and mend tools.	Ask an adult to put pest killer down in the feed shed, but keep it away from pets and small children.
	Clean out the feed shed (see page 17).	
	Check supplies.	
	Disinfect stable floor.	

BEDDING DOWN

Your pony needs a warm, comfortable bed in the stable so
he can lie down and rest. A deep bed also helps the pony
feel safe and stops him from hurting himself on the hard
floor. The pony's bed must be changed every day to keep it
clean. Making the bed is called bedding down.

CHOOSING THE BEDDING

There are several kinds of
suitable bedding for ponies.
Before you choose a
particular type, find out
how dusty it is. Dust is very
bad for ponies as it can
make them cough, which
keeps them from breathing
properly. You also need to
know the cost of the
bedding and how much you
will need. Make sure it is
easy to get fresh supplies,
and that you have
somewhere to store them
(see opposite).

*A deep straw bed like this one will help your pony to feel relaxed and
happy in his stable.*

SOME TYPES OF BEDDING YOU CAN USE

Bedding	Advantages	Disadvantages	Ways to get rid of it
Straw *Use wheat straw only as ponies eat other kinds.*	*Comfortable* *Dry* *Easy to get* *Cheap* *Easy to spread*	*Dusty - don't use if your pony tends to cough.*	*Burn it (but see below)* *Rots quickly* *Sell used straw and manure to mushroom growers.*
Wood shavings	*Not too dusty* *Absorbent* *Easy to use* *Pony can't eat them*	*Expensive* *Take a long time to rot*	*Might be used as compost for fields and gardens, so check first with friends and neighbors. May need to be burned.*
Shredded newspaper	*Dust free* *Absorbent* *Light and easy to lift*	*Hard to get* *Very light, so tends to blow around when you are mucking out.*	

HOW TO MAKE A BED FOR YOUR PONY

Take the pony out before you start.

Keep the door ajar to air the bed, and so you don't breathe in dust.

Put the fresh bedding ready in a wheelbarrow in the doorway.

Have the wheelbarrow handles pointing into the stable so you can wheel it out easily.

After mucking out, spread any leftover clean bedding across the stable floor. Shake it out well as you work, to get rid of any hard lumps that would make the bed uncomfortable for the pony to lie on.

Add fresh bedding with a fork. Undo the bale or bag inside the stable so it can't blow away. If you use straw, toss it first, to air it before spreading. Keep laying down bedding until the bed is ankle-deep.

Build the bed up higher around the walls. This keeps drafts out and encourages the pony to lie in the middle, where he won't get stuck in a corner if he rolls. If using shavings, make the top layer smooth.

USING A FORK

For laying a straw bed you need a four-pronged fork. The prongs are very sharp, so use it with care like this.

Keep the prongs down, away from your face.

Put your strongest hand in the lower position for a firmer grip. Have the other one near the top. Move the fork in a low arc, pushing the prongs away from you.

WHERE TO STORE BEDDING

It is cheaper to buy bedding in large amounts, so you need a big, dry storage space with room for a truck or tractor and trailer to park outside. A barn is ideal, but you could use an empty stable, shed or garage, as long as it has the features shown in the checklist (see right).

Put wooden pallets on the floor to stop the bedding from getting damp, and keep it neatly stacked. Check it often to make sure it is not rotting. To stop rats and mice from eating it, ask an adult to put poison under the pallets. Keep the storeroom shut so that young children and pets can't get in.

Storeroom checklist
* A roof and three walls to keep out rain and wind.
* It must be airy, with proper ventilation.
* Large entrance to let you in and out easily with bales or sacks.
* Set away from the stable as bedding is a big fire risk.
* If possible, it should have a lockable door for security.

MUCKING OUT

If your pony lives in for part or all of the time, you need to muck the stable out once a day. This means clearing all the droppings and dirty bedding out. You will also need to pick out once or twice a day. This is when you take away just the manure, so that the pony doesn't trample it into the bed.

TOOLS YOU NEED

A wheelbarrow to carry manure to the muck heap

A shavings fork for mucking out shavings

A four-pronged fork for mucking out straw

A broom with plastic or fiber bristles for sweeping the floor clear

A rubber or plastic tub (a laundry basket will do) for skepping out

A large, aluminum shovel for scooping up piles of manure

A hose for spraying muck off the floor now and then

Ideally, you should take your pony out of the stable when mucking out. If you can't, make sure he is securely tied out of your way.

DIFFERENT WAYS OF PICKING OUT

Your pony will produce a lot of droppings in a day, so it is very important to pick out regularly. This only takes about five minutes and you can leave the pony in the stable while you do it. Just move him over to one side.

To pick out a straw bed, use a fork to lift up any piles of droppings. Shake the fork over the tub so that the muck falls in with as little of the clean straw as possible.

To pick out shavings, it is quicker and easier to pick up the manure with your hands and drop it in the tub. Wear rubber gloves for this to protect your skin from germs.

HOW TO MUCK OUT THE STABLE

Clear the manure from the cleanest corner first so you can pile clean bedding there.

To stop the wind from blowing the dirty bedding away, put the wheelbarrow in the doorway.

Put the tools you need just outside the stable. Turn the pony loose in the field or tie him in the yard. Pick up dirty bedding and manure with the fork and put them in the wheelbarrow.

Fork all the clean bedding over to one side in a neat pile. You will reuse it when you make the pony's bed. Turn the bedding over as you work, making sure there is no manure underneath.

With the broom, sweep the floor. Let any wet patches dry. If the pony has to be inside while the floor is damp, put down a thin layer of bedding so he does not slip on the hard floor.

TOOL TIPS

* Store all tools in a safe, handy place out of the pony's reach but where you can get them easily.
* Never leave any tools lying around if the pony is anywhere near.
* Keep tools in good condition. Check them every week. Mend any broken parts at once.
* Use a four-pronged fork for straw. The prongs pick up bedding easily and break up any lumps.
* For shavings or newspaper, use a shavings fork to sort clean stuff from the rest. Its prongs work like a sieve.
* Sweep piles of dirty shavings onto the shovel with the broom. Ask a friend to hold the shovel while you sweep.

WHERE TO PUT THE MUCK

Horse manure doesn't smell too bad, but it is full of germs which are a health risk. It also attracts flies and pests like rats. You need a neat, safe muck heap where you can dump the droppings. It should be near enough so you don't have far to carry the muck, but far enough away so the smell and pests don't get into your home. If possible, have it near a track, so there is room for a tractor to get in and take the muck away.

Brick walls around three sides stop the muck from blowing away or falling down.

STABLE MANNERS AND VICES

Your pony may find living in a stable a little difficult at times. It's a small enclosed space, with little room for him to move around in. If he gets bored or bad-tempered he could be awkward or even dangerous to handle, so teach him good manners from the start and try to stop him from getting bored.

TEACHING STABLE MANNERS

Always be firm, quiet and confident when you handle a pony in the stable. Make sure you let him know you are coming by speaking, and shut the door after you as soon as you come in. Then approach him from the side, going to his shoulder so he can see you.

If you have work to do in the stable, always tie him up or take him out first to avoid accidents.

Always insist on good behavior when you enter the stable. To move your pony back from the door, gently push his chest with the flat of your hand. Say, "Back".

If he tries to push past and get out when you go in, put a bar across the doorway. This will stop him and help to break the habit.

To get him to move over in the stall, stand by his shoulder. Put your hand flat on his side and gently push, saying, "Over".

To make him stand still, tie him up. If he fidgets, say, "Stand". If he crowds you at feed time, say, "Back," then, "Stand". Make him wait until you fill the manger.

If he barges ahead when you bring him in, see if he has bashed himself on the gate. If he is just being pushy, put him in a bridle so that the bit gives you more control.

STABLE VICES

A pony that spends a lot of time in the stable is likely to get bored. Boredom leads to vices (bad habits) which can be impossible to cure once started, so it's important to keep a stabled pony happy.

Tips on preventing boredom
* Give him some time at pasture.
* Try to give him company, but don't stable him next to a pony he dislikes, as this will upset him.
* Keep the top half-door open so he can look out.
* Visit him often.
* Feed him regularly and always have some hay in his feeder.
* Even if you cannot ride him, take him out for a walk at least once a day.
* Give him a few toys, such as a plastic apple hung up so he can push it with his nose.
* Stick to a routine.

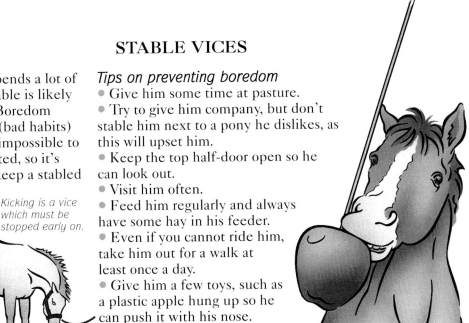

Kicking is a vice which must be stopped early on.

SOME COMMON VICES

Vice	What to look for	What you can do about it
Weaving	The pony swings his head from side to side in a continuous rhythm. He may lift each of his forelegs in turn from the ground as well. He may also stall walk, going around and around the stall.	Give him more exercise and try to turn him out more. You could fit a special anti-weave grill. This lets him look out, but stops him from rocking.
Biting	The pony flattens his ears, wrinkles his nose and bites you or others who try to handle him. Even nipping at your pockets for tidbits can develop into real biting, so watch out.	Never let a pony get away with biting. Tell him off at once by saying, "No" very firmly. If you must, give him one hard slap on the chest or shoulder, but never hit him on the head or he will become head-shy and even harder to handle. Don't give tidbits which only make him greedy and more likely to bite.
Cribbing and wind-sucking	He grips something like the edge of the stable door with his teeth. This can damage them and stop him from eating. Cribbing can develop into wind-sucking, where he also sucks in air.	Take out anything he might get hold of and paint the edge of the door with anti-chew fluid, or cover it with a metal chew strip.

FEEDING

Feeding is the most important part of how you look after your pony. It affects his health, behavior and looks. A well-fed pony is usually happy, relaxed and much easier to manage than one which is hungry or overfed.

HOW PONIES FEED AND WHAT THEY NEED

It is best to feed your pony in a similar way to how he would eat in the wild. Ponies have small stomachs in relation to their size, so they can only manage a little food at a time. At pasture, they graze for about 16 hours a day, eating small mouthfuls more or less continuously. This is called "trickle-feeding".

Ponies need bulk food, such as hay or grass, to fill them up and keep their digestion slow and steady. This makes them feel satisfied. They also need concentrated food, such as grain or oats, to give them energy for work.

How you combine the two types depends on how much work your pony does. The chart below shows how to get the right balance in his diet.

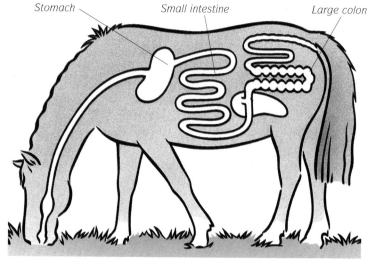

Stomach   Small intestine   Large colon

Small amounts of food move easily through your pony's complicated digestive system.

GETTING THE BALANCE RIGHT

What the pony is doing	Ratio of bulk to energy food
No work	*100% bulk: 0% concentrates*
Light work: *(short rides)*	*75% bulk: 25% concentrates*
Medium work: *(long rides, jumping, shows, eventing)*	*60% bulk: 40% concentrates*
Hard work: *(hunting)*	*50% bulk: 50% concentrates*

If you step up the amount of work your pony does, gradually increase the energy ration and reduce the bulk. Don't let the energizing food become more than half of the total food ration. This puts a strain on his digestion and makes the pony overexcited and difficult.

Feeding rules
* Feed according to pony's size, weight, age, work and temperament (see page 16).
* Feed little and often.
* Feed good quality food.
* Feed a succulent (grass, apples, carrots) every day.
* Feed at set times.
* Give the largest feeding at night so the pony has plenty to eat overnight.
* Avoid changes to diet. Make any changes slowly, over a few weeks.
* Keep feed buckets and mangers clean.
* Feed at least one-and-a-half hours before exercise.
* Let pony cool down after work before feeding him.

THE BEST FOOD FOR YOUR PONY

Hay is an excellent food. It is chewed and digested slowly and contains protein, fiber, calcium and vitamins. Good quality hay is the only food ponies need if they are not working. Choose meadow hay that is fresh and sweet-smelling. It should be four to eighteen months old.

The easiest way to make sure a working pony gets a balanced diet is to feed him compounds prepared by a specialist horse food manufacturer. If you feed hay or grass with them, compounds give the pony all the nourishment he needs. There are lots of different types, so you can choose one that suits him.

An easy way to feed your pony compounds is to give him pony pellets. These are made of various ingredients ground up, dried and then made into pellets.

TYPES OF FOOD

Energy foods	Bulk foods	Other
Several types of grain can be fed as part of the diet. **Oats**: very nourishing but can make ponies fat and overexcited (called "heating" effect). **Barley**: not widely used but good for putting weight on a pony in poor shape. **Corn**: very heating. Fattening, so only use as a small part of diet.	**Dried sugar-beet pulp**: has to be soaked for 24 hours before use so does not choke pony. Full of energy but non-heating. Tasty, useful for dampening feed. **Hay**: very healthy food. Fills pony up and keeps him chewing slowly. **Grass**: fresh grass added to the feeding is a nourishing treat. Never feed grass clippings, which are poisonous.	**Carrots and apples**: feed raw, washed and sliced. Help digestion and appetite. **Linseed and linseed cake**: full of protein and oil. Makes coat shine. Linseed must be soaked and cooked or it is poisonous.

HOW MUCH TO FEED YOUR PONY

The amount of food your pony needs depends on how big he is, how much work he does, his age and character. If he is mainly at pasture, he will sometimes need extra food, depending on the weather and how much grass there is. Each pony is an individual, so it's impossible to say exactly how much to give all ponies. The chart below gives you an idea of the quantities involved and how to split up the feedings each day.

Grazing freely stops ponies from getting bored. Moving about, or foraging for food like this, is also very good for their digestion.

SAMPLE FEEDING CHART AND TIMETABLE

Size of pony, work he does, where he lives	Approx. weight of pony	Total feed per day	A.M.	Lunch	P.M.
13.2 hh *light work; mainly stabled*	*350 kg (770lbs)*	*8kg (17.5lbs)*	*3.5kg (7.75lbs) hay; 0.5kg (1lb) grain*	*If possible, turn out for a few hours*	*3.5kg. (7.75lbs) hay; 0.5kg (1lb) grain*
13.2hh; *light work; mainly on pasture*	*350 kg*	*8kg*	*Summer: grass; 0.5kg (1lb) grain* *Winter: 3.5kg (7.75lbs) hay; 0.5kg (1lb) grain*		*Summer: grass; 0.5kg (1lb) grain* *Winter: 3.5kg (7.75lbs) 0.5kg (1lb) grain*
14.2hh; *medium work; mainly stabled*	*420kg (925lbs)*	*9kg (20lbs)*	*3.2kg (7lbs) hay; 1.3kg (3lbs) grain*	*If possible, turn out for a few hours*	*3.2kg (7lbs) hay; 1.3kg (3lbs) grain*
14.2hh; *medium work; mainly on pasture*	*420kg*	*9kg*	*Summer: grass; 1.3kg (3lbs) grain* *Winter: 3.2kg (7lbs) hay; 1.3kg (3lbs) grain*		*Summer: grass; 1.3kg (3lbs) grain* *Winter: 3.2kg (7lbs) hay; 1.3kg (3lbs) grain*

STORING AND SERVING FOOD

Ponies are fussy feeders and won't eat food that tastes bad or stale, so only buy about one week's supply and store it in air-tight feed bins that keep it dry and safe from mice and rats. Don't put fresh food on top of stale or old batches. Always empty the bin first.

Keep all feeding equipment clean with regular scrubbing and rinsing (the photograph on the right shows you what you need).

If you can, store the food in a separate shed. It is especially important to keep it out of the tack room, as mice that are drawn to the food will also eat leather. It's best to store hay in a high, airy barn. Make sure it's bone-dry when stored.

Weighing scales are essential as you need to know exactly how much you give at each feeding.

A haynet could be handy for weighing hay and is used for traveling and at shows.

Feed bins should be tough plastic or metal, with tight-fitting lids, so they are completely rodent-proof.

Mangers are useful for keeping food tidy and preventing waste.

Metal or plastic scoops are best for measuring out the dry food.

GIVING YOUR PONY WATER

Make sure your pony can drink as and when he needs to. This keeps him from drinking a lot at one time, which can cause colic. In the stable, use an automatic water bowl, or give a fresh bucketful at least four times a day, and two for the night.

An automatic water bowl refills as soon as the pony drinks out of it.

Rules of watering

* Keep water always available.
* Make sure the water and containers are fresh and clean.
* Don't let ponies drink from ponds or unused troughs where the water is stagnant and dirty.
* Don't let ponies drink from streams with sandy beds. Sand causes colic (see page 31).
* Always offer water before a feeding.
* During a long ride, give him small amounts often, rather than one big drink.
* Don't give large amounts of cold water straight after exercise. Instead, as long as he isn't puffing, give him a small drink while he cools off. This will stop him from getting dehydrated.
* Pour away any water that has manure or urine in it at once.
* Match the amount of water to your pony's needs. These will vary depending on how much work he is doing and how hot it is.

GROOMING

It is essential to groom your pony regularly, not just to make him look good, but to help him stay healthy. A stabled pony needs a full grooming every day, as he can't roll around to groom himself.

WHAT GROOMING IS FOR

Grooming keeps your pony's skin and coat in good condition. In the wild, his coat would naturally suit his needs and the season of the year (see page 24), but a pony who lives in and is ridden needs extra help.

By brushing his coat, you get the dirt and oil out of the pores (tiny holes) in his skin, which means he can sweat freely. Grooming also helps the blood under his skin to flow well, which is another way of keeping him fit. Lastly, brushing and rubbing his coat makes it stay smooth and glossy.

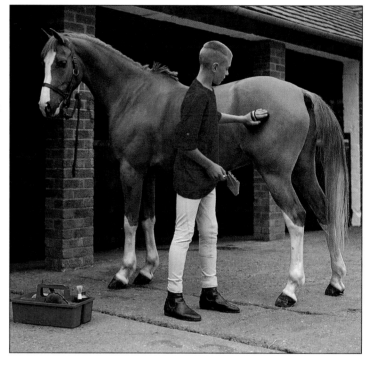

THE GROOMING KIT

Dandy brush for brushing off mud. Has long stiff bristles.

Body brush removes oil and dirt. Has shorter, softer bristles.

Stable cloth polishes coat to make it glossy.

Stiff brush for brushing hooves (see page 22).

Mane comb for thinning or "pulling" mane and tail.

Rubber curry comb for brushing off mud and shedding hair.

Metal curry comb for cleaning body brush. Never use it on the pony!

Three sponges, one each for wiping:
- eyes
- lips and nostrils
- dock (bottom).
Make sure each looks different.

Hoof pick for cleaning dirt and stones out of the feet.

Hoof oil for sealing and protecting the feet.

Sweat scraper for scraping off sweat and water.

GIVING YOUR PONY A FULL GROOMING

Tie the pony in a warm sheltered place.

Brush along the natural lie of the coat.

Scrape brush with curry comb to get oil off.

Tie the pony up. If you are in the stable, pick it out so the pony won't tread in any manure. Then pick out the feet, being careful not to hurt the frog (see page 22). Check for any wounds.

Take off or fold back any blankets. Stand sideways to the pony, facing his tail and beside his neck. Brush lightly all over the neck and body with the dandy brush. Don't brush the head.

Then take the body brush in one hand and the metal curry comb in the other. Brush the pony firmly all over, leaning on the brush so it pushes through the coat to the skin.

To do the head, put the curry comb down and untie the pony so he doesn't pull back. Hold him by the nose as you gently body brush his head. Tie him up again.

Push the mane over to the "wrong" side of the neck. Body brush the exposed skin. Using a damp sponge, bring the mane back over in small sections.

Standing to one side, lift the tail and hold it out from the hindquarters. Brush it through, bit by bit, starting with the undermost layer. Brush down to the ends.

Carefully sponge the eyes with a little warm water. Change the water, then sponge the nose and lips. Wipe the dock with the dock sponge.

Polish the coat with the stable cloth to bring out its natural shine. Finish by painting each hoof inside and out with hoof oil (see pages 22-23).

Grooming tips
* Groom soon after riding, once pony is dry. Skin is warm with open pores, so dirt comes off easily.
* Store grooming kit in a waterproof box.
* Don't use kit on more than one pony, as this spreads germs.
* Clean brushes weekly in a solution of dish soap and water. Rinse and dry.

DEALING WITH WET OR MUDDY PONIES

Your pony's coat needs to be completely dry before you groom him, otherwise dirt and oil won't come out. If he lives at pasture, you should also dry him thoroughly before turning him out, or he may get a chill. After riding, always walk him for a while to cool down. Then dry him off like this.

Rub him dry with an old, clean towel before putting his blanket on. Make sure no moisture is trapped under there, or it could make him cold.

If he is very wet, get water off with the sweat scraper. Then cover his back and quarters with fresh straw and fasten a blanket on. This is called "thatching".

Hose muddy legs clean with warm water, then dry them. This stops the risk of scratches (see page 31). Let mud on the body dry, then brush it off.

GROOMING PASTURE-KEPT PONIES

A pony at pasture should not be groomed very much, as the oil in his coat keeps him warm and dry. Most of the time, you only need to dandy brush him lightly before you ride. Get any mud off the saddle area and where the girth goes to stop it from rubbing and causing sores. Make sure these parts are dry.

Don't use a body brush, except on the head, mane and tail, as it takes oil out of the coat. Pick out and check the feet carefully, then sponge the face and dock. If your pony has a thick coat, feel through it to make sure he is not too thin underneath.

Ponies at pasture groom themselves naturally by rolling, or by rubbing against a fence. They also groom each other, using their lips and teeth like this.

EXTRA GROOMING

You can help to keep your pony in good shape by giving his biggest muscles an extra rubdown now and then. These are the ones that he works the most. The picture on the right shows you which ones to rub. It's best to give the pony his usual grooming first (see page 19). Then use the stable cloth to rub him down. He will probably enjoy it, but stop if he fidgets.

Hindquarters

Top of neck

Shoulder muscle

Pony should stand with weight balanced on all four legs

PULLING THE MANE AND TAIL

You need to thin out, or "pull", the mane and tail every six weeks so they don't grow too bushy. It doesn't hurt the pony - his hair is much less sensitive than yours. Mane pulling is easier after exercise, when the pores of the skin are open.

To work on the mane, split it into small sections. Comb down the hairs in each section.

Hold the longest hairs and push the rest back with the comb. Tweak out the long hairs.

Only pull the top of the tail. Drape it over the stable door so you are safe if the pony kicks.

QUARTERING: A QUICK GROOMING

If your pony lives inside, he may get dirty from lying in a mucky bed. Before riding out, you can clean him up quickly without taking his blanket off. This is called "quartering". Tie the pony up, fold the front half of his blanket back, and body brush his front. Fold the blanket back down. Do the same for his hindquarters. Use a damp dock sponge to get muck stains off, and dry wet patches with a stable cloth. Body brush and clean the face as usual. Pick stray bedding from the mane and tail and brush them. Wipe the dock, then carefully pick out the feet (see page 22), checking for loose nails.

Just undo the blanket and fold part of it back. Keep it on so that the pony stays warm.

HOOFCARE AND SHOEING

Your pony's hooves are very important. They support his weight and take the shock of his movements. You need to look after them very carefully and be able to tell if they are healthy or not. You also need a good farrier to trim them and fit horseshoes.

THE STRUCTURE OF THE HOOF

Hooves, like fingernails and hair, grow all the time, so they need regular trimming. The outer wall is hard and doesn't feel things, which is why shoeing doesn't hurt the pony. The sole is made of hard horn, but has a tender area beneath.

The frog acts as a gripper and absorbs the shock of movement.

The white line is a layer of soft horn between the wall and sole. Farrier uses it to judge how far nails can go so they don't pierce sole.

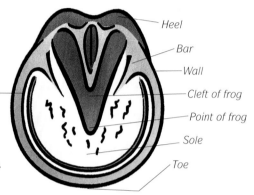

Heel
Bar
Wall
Cleft of frog
Point of frog
Sole
Toe

LOOKING AFTER YOUR PONY'S FEET

You should pick out and check your pony's feet at least once a day, and two or three times if he is stabled and standing in a bed that may be damp and dirty. Always pick the feet out before and after a ride. Each time, check the feet inside and out as well. Tie the pony up to handle his feet, and then follow the steps on the right.

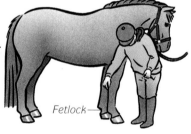

Fetlock

Run your hand down his leg to the fetlock. Grasp it and lift up, saying "Up." Lean on him so he shifts his weight off the foot.

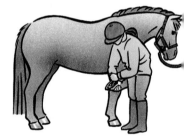

Work from heel to toe, with the hoofpick pointing away from you. Scrape out all the dirt. Brush the frog gently with a hoof brush.

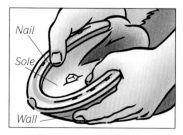

Nail
Sole
Wall

Check the sole for bruises or wounds, and the wall for cracks. See if the shoes are worn out. Check no nails are loose or sticking out.

Brush should be wet but not dripping.

Hooves need moisture to grow and stop them from cracking. Brush them inside and out sometimes with a stiff, wet brush.

Hoof oil

Use a paintbrush.

Oiling the feet seals in the moisture and makes them look good. Put plenty on the sole, so it soaks in. Then do the outside.

WHEN DOES MY PONY NEED SHOES?

In the wild, ponies wear their feet down naturally as they roam. When ridden on hard surfaces, they need iron shoes to stop the hoof walls from wearing out too fast, and making their feet sore and damaged. With shoes on, the feet don't wear down naturally, so they need to be trimmed every four to six weeks.

The shoes may also need to be replaced. Make sure you get a qualified farrier for this work.

Try to get the same one each time as he will get to know exactly what your pony needs. Make sure your pony is ready when he comes. Bring him in, wash and dry his feet and legs and pick out his hooves. Prepare a hard, clean surface for him to stand on, preferably outside, where there is plenty of light.

WHAT WILL THE FARRIER DO?

When you call the farrier, tell him whether your pony needs a set of brand-new shoes, or just the existing ones taken off, his feet trimmed, and the old shoes put back on.

When the farrier arrives, have your pony ready in a halter so you can hold him while the farrier works. The farrier may also ask you to lead your pony up and down so that he can see how he moves.

First, the farrier loosens the nails in the shoes. He can then take them off with pincers like this without tearing the pony's feet.

Good fit checklist
Before the farrier leaves, check that your pony's shoes fit properly. This list will help.
* Shoe must fit hoof, not hoof over-rasped to fit shoe.
* Shoe is the right weight and type for the pony.
* Hoof walls trimmed neatly.
* Clenches (nail tips) evenly spaced and level on hoof wall.
* Nailheads fit tightly in holes on shoe.
* No gaps between hoof and shoe.
* Heels of shoes cover heels of feet.
* Six to eight nails per shoe, depending on the pony and the farrier.

Next, he trims each foot, and lightly rasps the soles so that they are even. He looks closely at the shape and condition of the feet.

Then he either puts the old shoes back on, or fits new ones. The shoes are nailed into the hard, nerveless rim of the hoof.

CLIPPING

For winter, your pony grows a thick, waterproof coat to keep him warm. If you are going to work him hard, it might be a good idea to have him clipped, but only if you have a heavy blanket and a stable. Clipping will prevent him from getting too hot and sweaty when he works, which could make him tired and ill. Never clip a pony yourself: it's a skilled job, so get an expert to do it.

WHEN AND WHAT TYPE OF CLIP

Your pony's winter coat starts to grow from about September, so his first clip should be in October once most of this has grown in. After clipping, the coat goes on growing for a while, so he may need a second clip in December if he does a lot of work. Make sure you don't clip him after January, because that is when he grows his light coat for the summer, which doesn't need clipping. He should always have the right amount of coat to suit his work and the season.

The more work he does, the less coat he should have (but he will have to wear a blanket when he's resting). Below are three common types of clip.

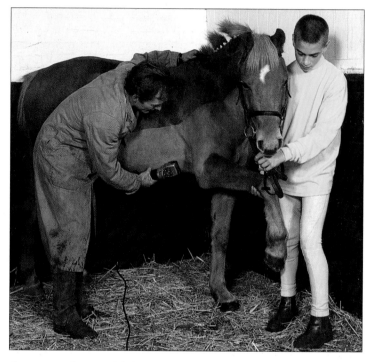

If your pony lives outside he needs plenty of coat left on. He may just need a trace clip. Ideally, you should wear a hard hat when helping.

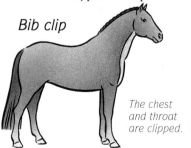

Bib clip

The chest and throat are clipped.

Trace clip

The flanks and belly are done, too.

Blanket clip

Hair is left on the loins, back and legs.

This type is ideal if the pony lives outside and does light work. He can winter out and may not need to be blanketed.

This is fine for a hardy pony who winters out but is being competed. He will need a full, heavy blanket when resting.

This type allows a hard-working pony to keep cool. He must be stabled at night, and fully blanketed when not being ridden.

GETTING READY FOR CLIPPING

Two to three weeks before clipping, start working your pony so he sweats lightly, which keeps his coat clean. Keep him well groomed. Make sure you have the blankets he needs and that they fit (see pages 26-27). They should be clean and ready to use. You will need one to keep the pony warm during clipping.

On the day checklist
* Tie the pony's mane in rubber bands. Groom him so he is clean and dry.
* Put up his bed and sweep the floor. Let it dry. Put straw down, or rubber matting if you have it.
* Make sure stall is well-lit and free from drafts.
* Remove water from stall to avoid electric shocks.

* If you are helping, wear close-fitting clothes, and tie long hair back so nothing gets caught in the clippers.
* Wear rubber-soled shoes to reduce the risk of shocks, and a hard hat for safety.

HOW A PONY IS TRACE CLIPPED

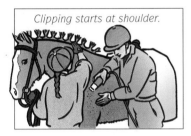

Clipping starts at shoulder.

So the pony doesn't startle at the sudden noise and feel of the clippers, they are first turned on away from him, then turned off and lain on his shoulder. They are then taken off, switched on again, and part of his neck is clipped.

Once the pony settles down, the flanks and belly are done. The clippers are always worked against the lie of the coat. You can help by holding each of the front legs forward in turn, so the skin doesn't get caught in the clippers.

The top half of the neck and the hairs under his head are done last, when he is really settled, so he is less likely to act up about clippers near his head. You can help to soothe him by putting your hand on his nose and speaking to him.

CARING FOR A CLIPPED PONY

Once your pony is clipped, body brush him to massage his skin and get oil and loose hair off. Check that he hasn't been nicked by the clippers. Shake his blanket out and put it back on.

Brush out his mane and tail and wipe his face and dock to get hairs off. If he lives outside, put him in a blanket (see page 26). Make sure he has shelter (see page 4).

If his head is clipped, a hood will keep him snug and warm.

BLANKETS

Blankets are used to keep ponies warm if they have had their coats clipped, or live outside all through the winter. A blanket is also useful if a pony is very wet, as it helps him get warm and dry off more quickly. Blankets also protect a pony's coat and keep it looking good.

NEW ZEALAND BLANKETS

As long as they have shelter, ponies that live outside most of the year only need a New Zealand blanket. This is a very hard-wearing, waterproof canvas or nylon blanket which fastens with straps across the pony's chest and between his hindlegs, so that it doesn't come off or stop him from moving freely. If you can, have two so that you can keep a clean, spare one for when the other gets wet and dirty in bad weather.

OTHER TYPES OF BLANKETS

A stable blanket is warm and quilted. It is easy to wash and can be worn day and night. It is suitable for a pony who lives in most of the time and is clipped in winter. You can buy these blankets in different weights and thicknesses.

A sweat sheet is made of mesh so that the air or sweat can evaporate through the holes. You can put it under a summer sheet (see right) to let a hot, sweaty pony cool off gradually, without catching a chill.

A summer sheet is a lightweight cotton or linen sheet. It's good for keeping flies and dust off a stabled, groomed pony, or for protecting a pasture-kept pony from insects in hot weather. It's handy for traveling to shows, too.

HOW TO PUT ON A NEW ZEALAND BLANKET

Blanket should lie straight and flat.

Tie the pony up. Fold the blanket into quarters and stand with it at the pony's left shoulder. Stroke him so he knows you are there. Gently put the blanket on his back and unfold it.

The blanket should cover the withers at the front, and the quarters at the back. Stand behind the pony, slightly to one side. Check that the middle seam lies along the spine.

If the blanket is too far forward, pull it toward the tail. If it is too far back, lift it rather than pulling it, so that you don't rub the pony's hair in the wrong direction under the blanket.

Blanketing tips
* Before buying, measure pony from middle of chest to under tail. Give details to saddler who will tell you the size you need.
* Choose the best quality blanket you can afford.
* Check blanket twice a day to see straps are fastened, it has not slipped or torn, and isn't rubbing.
* At night, take off blanket, shake it out, then reblanket so pony is comfortable.

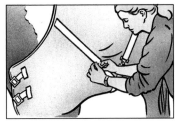

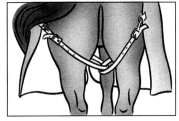

When the blanket is in place, fasten the surcingles (the straps around his belly) so the blanket will stay on if he moves. Buckle the chest straps, making sure they are not too tight.

Next, buckle the leg straps. Fasten the left one around the left leg, then thread the right strap through the left before fastening it around the right leg. This stops the blanket from slipping.

A WELL-FITTING BLANKET

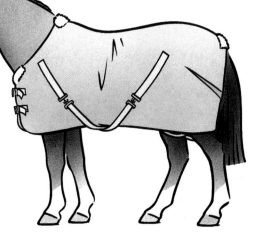

Reaches in front of the withers.

Fits snugly around the shoulders so it doesn't slip back and cut into the withers.

Is not too tight around the neck. It must not press on the throat even when the pony puts his neck down to graze.

Wraps under the girth without wrinkling the skin at the elbows.

Is not too long. It mustn't drag backward or it presses on the throat and spine.

Is long enough at the sides to cover the pony's flanks.

Reaches the top of the tail.

CLEANING TACK

It's important to clean your tack regularly; if possible, after every ride. It must be washed, dried and rubbed with saddle soap to keep it supple. Never use ordinary soap, which makes leather dry and stiff. If you are pushed for time, you can just wipe it over with a damp cloth, as long as you clean the bit properly, and clean everything thoroughly once a week.

WHAT YOU NEED

Two sponges, one for washing and one for soaping the leather

A bar of saddle soap

A bucket for water

A chamois leather for drying the leather

Metal polish and a cloth for applying polish

A cloth for buffing (rubbing the metal until it shines)

A stable cloth or dish towel for holding the metal parts so you don't smudge them

A blunt knife for getting off blobs of oil or caked dirt

A matchstick for getting soap out of buckle holes

WASHING TACK

To wash the saddle, put it on a saddle rack and take off the girth, stirrup leathers and irons, and buckleguards. Never put it in water: this makes the stuffing all lumpy. Wipe it all over with a damp sponge dipped in warm water. Dry it with a chamois. Scrub fabric girths with mild soap and water. Rinse well.

Take the bridle apart. Wash each piece with a damp sponge, and dry it.

CLEANING METAL

You need to wash and then polish the metal parts, except for the bit, which should only be washed. Take the stirrup irons off their leathers, pull the treads out and wash the dirt off with warm soapy water. Dry them, then put the polish on. Buff them with the clean cloth to make them shine. Put the treads back in and fasten the irons on to the leathers. Take the bit off the bridle and wash it thoroughly in very hot water. Don't use soap, or your pony will get upset by the taste when you put the bit in his mouth. Dry it carefully.

Cleaning your tack is a good chance to check it for wear and tear, too.

SOAPING THE SADDLE AND BRIDLE

Put the dry saddle on the saddle rack. Dip the soap in warm water, then rub it on the soaping sponge. This should be just damp so you don't get too much foam on the sponge.

Don't dip the sponge in the water.

Moving the sponge in small circles, rub soap into the whole saddle. Resoap the sponge as you go. Make sure saddle parts that touch the pony, such as the flaps, are well soaped.

Do the underside of the flaps too.

Cover the saddle with a clean dish towel and hang it on a saddle bracket on the wall. Then soap the stirrup leathers and the girth if it is leather. Hang all these up to dry.

Lay all the pieces of the bridle out neatly on a clean table and put the bit to one side (remember not to soap this). Put some saddle soap on your damp sponge as you did before.

Starting with the headpiece, wrap the sponge around each strap. Grip it firmly, and pull the sponge down the strap several times in a strong, stroking movement.

When each piece is done, put the bridle back together (see right). Check that hooks face in and buckles face out, and that the noseband is inside the cheekpieces.

Hang bridle up once it is cleaned.

PUTTING THE BRIDLE BACK TOGETHER

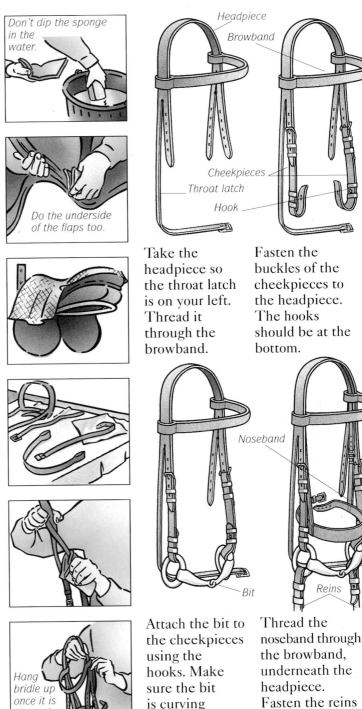

Headpiece
Browband
Cheekpieces
Throat latch
Hook
Noseband
Bit
Reins

Take the headpiece so the throat latch is on your left. Thread it through the browband.

Fasten the buckles of the cheekpieces to the headpiece. The hooks should be at the bottom.

Attach the bit to the cheekpieces using the hooks. Make sure the bit is curving upward.

Thread the noseband through the browband, underneath the headpiece. Fasten the reins to the bit.

29

HEALTH AND FIRST AID

To keep your pony healthy, visit him twice a day, and make sure you check him over at least once daily. As you get to know him, you will soon be able to tell if he is not well. It's always worth calling the vet if you're worried, but it helps if you already know how to recognize signs of illness (some common ones are shown opposite). Make sure you also have a good first aid kit.

IN GOOD HEALTH

A healthy pony looks alert and at ease with himself. He has bright, clear eyes, and he pricks and moves his ears whenever he hears a sound. He should look neither too lean or "ribby", nor so fat that he can't get around without puffing. His coat should look sleek and shiny when groomed.

Signs of illness
* Head droops.
* Body held awkwardly, or "tucked up".
* Ears lying flat and still.
* Dull eyes with bright red rims.
* Discharge from nostrils or eyes.
* Dull coat with no shine or "bloom".
* Sweating or shivering when he hasn't been worked.
* Tail tucked into body.
* Lack of interest in surroundings.
* Doesn't eat properly.
* Hot or swollen limbs.
* No droppings passed, or sloppy droppings.

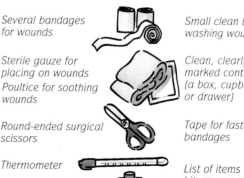

This pony shows all the signs of good health: gleaming eyes, ears pricked forward, a glossy coat and lots of bounding energy.

FIRST AID KIT

Gauze bandage for dressing wounds

Cotton for cleaning wounds

Antiseptic solution, cream or powder, for putting on wounds

Petroleum jelly for when you use the thermometer, and for bald patches on skin

Several bandages for wounds

Sterile gauze for placing on wounds
Poultice for soothing wounds

Round-ended surgical scissors

Thermometer

Fly repellent

Small clean bucket for washing wounds

Clean, clearly marked container (a box, cupboard or drawer)

Tape for fastening bandages

List of items in the kit, so you can check that you have them

COLIC

Illness	Causes	Signs	What to do
This is very bad tummy ache. Colic can usually be cured very quickly with medication, but you should call the vet at once if you think your pony has it. If the pony tries to roll to stop the pain, he can twist his gut and die.	It can come from overfeeding, or from having worms, or from exercising the pony right after feeding him.	Sweating Swishing tail Biting or kicking at belly with hind foot Pawing the ground Rolling or trying to roll a lot Unsettled, shifting from foot to foot, groaning	Call the vet at once If pony is lying still, don't move him If he is restless or thrashes around, keep him moving gently and keep him warm. Don't let him roll

LAMINITIS

Illness	Causes	Signs	What to do
This is a very painful fever in the feet caused by inflammation in the tender parts just behind the hoof wall. Laminitis needs to be treated by a vet, especially as it may keep coming back if it goes untreated for too long.	It happens if the pony eats too much rich grass or concentrates, which can release poisons into the blood which stop it from circulating properly in the feet. Cross-section view of hoof This part becomes inflamed	Very hot, painful hooves Pony moves unevenly, becoming very lame as illness worsens Pony stands with his front legs stuck stiffly out, taking his weight on his heels May run a temperature Seems upset and very restless	Call the vet Only give hay and water Soak feet in cold water Make a deep shavings bed which is soft on the feet but pony can't eat

SCRATCHES

Illness	Causes	Signs	What to do
This is a nasty illness where the skin on the heels cracks, gets infected and the cracking spreads up the legs. These become hot, swollen and covered in scabs. In bad cases, scratches can cause lameness. You can prevent it if you make sure your pony is on well-drained land if he lives outside. Cover his legs with barrier cream.	Standing on muddy, damp ground for long periods chaps the skin. It then gets sore and scabby, the hair falls out and germs get in through the wounds, causing scratches.	Skin on heels gets red, tender and cracked Hot, swollen legs Scabs on legs	Wash affected skin with warm, medicated water Dry very thoroughly May need to clip hair off the affected area Ask vet about which ointment to apply If bad, get vet to see pony

INDEX

USEFUL ADDRESSES

American Horse Show Association, Inc.
Suite 409
220 East 42nd St.
New York, NY 10017
USA.

Canadian Equestrian Federation
1600 James Naismith
Drive, Gloucester,
Ontario,
K1B 5N4,
Canada.

The British Equestrian Centre
Stoneleigh, Kenilworth
Warwickshire
CV8 2LR
England
(**The Pony Club** is also at
this address)

Equestrian Federation of Australia Inc.
52 Kensington Rd,
Rose Park,
S. Australia, 5067

New Zealand Equestrian Federation
P.O. Box 47,
Hastings, Hawke's Bay,
New Zealand.

With thanks to Chloe Albert, Glenn Whitbread, Nayla Ammar, Stephanie Sarno, all the staff and
ponies at Trent Park Equestrian Centre, and Coleman Croft Master Saddlers.